British Library Cataloguing in Publication Data

Hately, David
    The Christmas robin.
    I. Title   II. Barr, Noel : Wise robin
    III. Stevenson, Peter, *1953-*   IV. Series
    823'.914 J
    ISBN 0-7214-9585-0

First edition

Published by Ladybird Books Ltd Loughborough Leicestershire UK
Ladybird Books Inc Auburn Maine 04210 USA

© LADYBIRD BOOKS LTD MCMLXXXVIII

Printed in England

The Christmas Robin

Adapted by David Hately from
The Wise Robin by Noel Barr
Illustrated by Peter Stevenson

Ladybird Books

It was cold, very cold, and snow lay thick on the ground. Mr Robin searched in vain for food. He couldn't find any insects to eat, because they were hiding away from the cold. He couldn't go digging for worms, because the ground was too icy and hard.

At last, cold and hungry, he gave up and flew back to his nest.

Mrs Robin was hungry, too. ''Is there anything for supper?'' she asked.

Mr Robin shook his head. He tried to say ''No,'' but it came out as ''Brrr''.

''Never mind,'' said Mrs Robin cheerfully. ''Perhaps we'll have better luck tomorrow.''

But the next day was even colder, and still Mr Robin could find nothing to eat.

Mr Robin decided to search for food in the garden of a nearby house. Suddenly there was a noise from the house. With a tweet of alarm, Mr Robin hid behind a snowman.

Peeping round, he saw a window being opened. A hand scattered something on the windowsill.

When all was quiet again, Mr Robin flew up to the window to investigate.

Perching on the windowsill, Mr Robin saw some neat little holes in the snow. He stuck his beak down one of the holes and could hardly believe his luck when he found a juicy currant.

As well as currants, there were cake crumbs and bread. There was even some toasted tea cake!

Mr Robin hurried back to Mrs Robin and together they returned to the windowsill, where they enjoyed a delicious supper.

When they had finished, Mrs Robin peered in through the window, twisting her head this way and that to get a better view.

Suddenly she gasped. "Look!" she said. "There's a fir tree growing inside this house!"

The Robins had never seen a tree like it. At its top was a bright star, and hanging from the branches were twinkling fairy lights, coloured balls of shining glass, crackers and bags of nuts and sweets.

There were also some long pieces of glittering tinsel.

"Look at that silver moss!" breathed Mrs Robin. "Isn't it beautiful?"

Later that evening, when they were back in their nest, Mrs Robin said, "Wouldn't our nest look lovely with some of that silver moss woven in among the twigs? Will you get some for me, dear?"

Mr Robin gulped. He was afraid that if he went into the house he might get caught, but he couldn't bear to disappoint Mrs Robin. "Of course I will. I'll get some for you tomorrow," he said, trying to sound brave. "Now let's get some sleep."

Next morning, Mr Robin flew over to the windowsill.
There was no one in the room and the window was
open. He fluttered in and settled on a branch of the tree.

Suddenly the door burst open and into the room came
two large people and two small ones.

"Happy Christmas, Matthew and Charlotte!" said the two large people. "Choose a present from the Christmas tree."

Mr Robin shivered with fright and tried to hide behind a cracker.

The little person called Matthew asked for some sweets. But the one called Charlotte pointed to Mr Robin and cried, "I want the toy robin!"

"But I'm not a toy!" thought
Mr Robin. "I'm a real, live
robin!" And just as a big hand
reached up to lift him from the tree,
he sprang to the top branch, threw
back his head, and started to sing
at the top of his voice. As he trilled
and whistled and chirruped, the
people clapped their hands.

When he had finished his song Mr Robin flew out of the window and hopped down onto the windowsill.

Charlotte ran across the room. ''Thank you, little robin,'' she said, ''for making this the best Christmas tree ever. Come and see us again!''

When Mrs Robin heard what had happened she forgot all about the tinsel. ''As long as you're safe,'' she said, ''that's all that matters.''

But twelve days after his adventure, Mr Robin found the fir tree lying near the dustbins. Caught on its branches were some scraps of tinsel.

Mr Robin took them back to decorate the nest. Mrs Robin was overjoyed! She had her silver moss after all!